Milly Molly®

B O O K S

22 November 2013

This Milly, Molly book belongs to

Lilly Saville

To dear wee Lilly
Grandad & Ami hope you
enjoy this book.

x x x

For my grandchildren

Thomas, Harry, Ella and Madeleine.

Milly, Molly and Sock Heaven

Copyright © Milly Molly Books, 2002

Gill Pittar and Cris Morrell assert the moral right to
be recognised as the author and illustrator of this work.

Published by
Milly Molly Books
P O Box 539
Gisborne, New Zealand
email: books@millymolly.com

Printed by Rhythm Consolidated Berhad, Malaysia

ISBN: 1-877297-26-7

10   9   8   7   6   5   4   3   2   1

Milly, Molly
and
Sock Heaven

"We may look different
but we feel the same."

Milly's dad was desperate. "I'll hug anyone who can find my missing sock. Anyone!" he said.

He had been through the clothesbasket,

looked in the washing machine

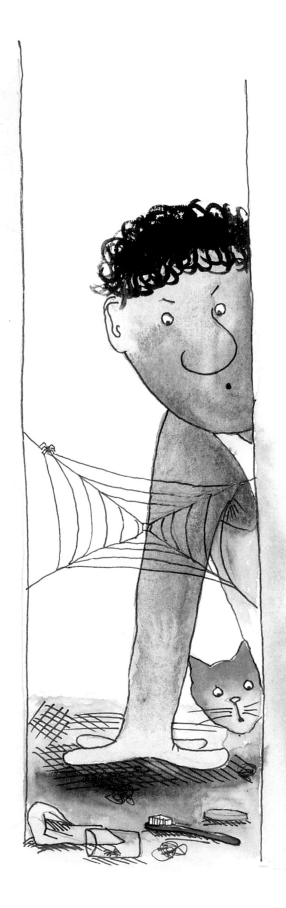

and down behind the drier.

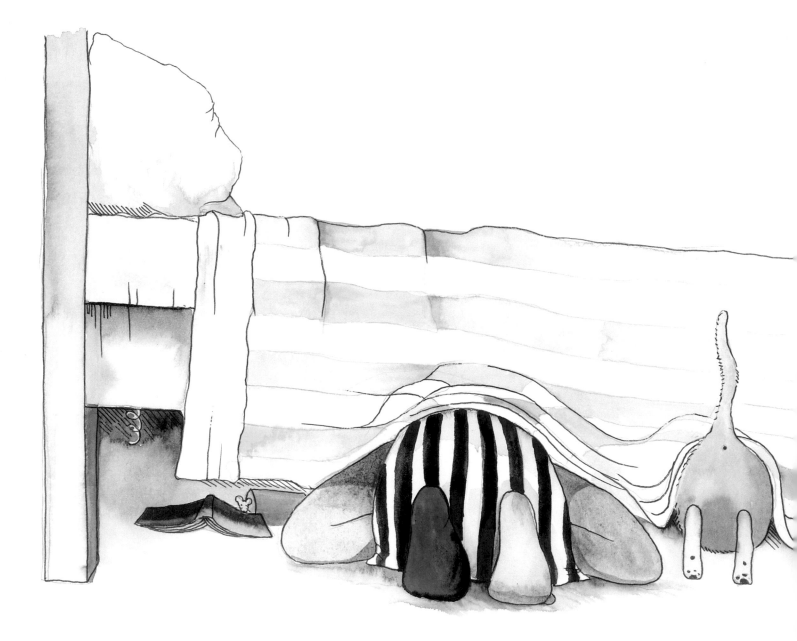

He had looked under his bed

and in the toe of his gumboots.

He had turned his sock drawer over twice

and searched high and low.

Milly and Molly had never seen him so miserable. And they'd never heard him say he would hug just anyone. That was the bit that worried them the most.

Who had gone off with his sock?

They checked out the postman.

They asked Aunt Maude politely to lift her skirt.

They pleaded with Old Frosty to stretch up and pick them an apple.

The butcher's socks came up to his knees

and Mr Limpy said, "I have a similar problem".

Miss Blythe said, "socks make my feet itchy".

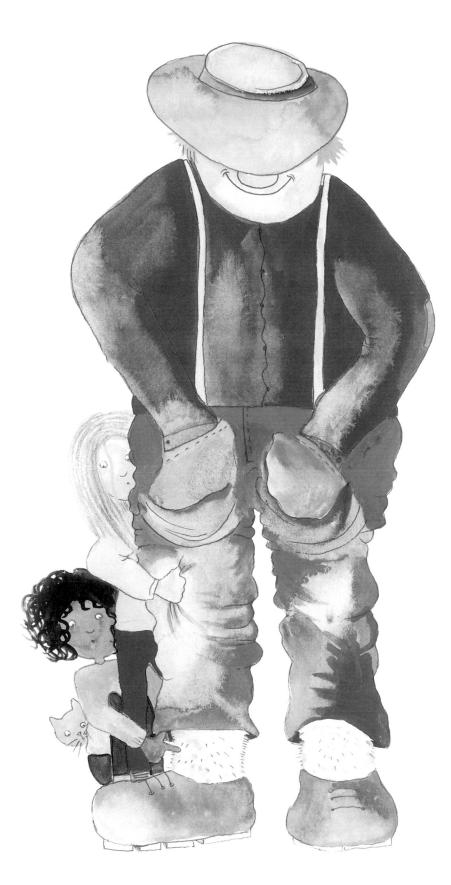

And Farmer Hegarty's socks looked far too big and woolly.

Doctor Smiley's socks were black.

BushBob's socks were stripey.

Father Brownlie said, "I don't wear socks and, besides, everyone knows socks don't go missing. They just collect in sock heaven".

Molly's mother said, "I haven't seen a blue sock in the wash".

And Milly's mother said, "I've never known anyone to lose more socks. I'll bet it's still in his sock drawer!"

Late that night Milly's dad turned out the lights and put Marmalade to bed.

And there it was! His blue sock. He told
Marmalade she was the best cat and gave
her a great, big hug.